A CASCADE OF FATES

ERIC MAWSON

Eric Mawson's critically acclaimed Trilogy Of Fates is now followed up by his exciting new book A Cascade of Fates. Soon to be made into two major motion pictures.

A CASCADE OF FATES

ERIC MAWSON

CITIOFBOOKS, INC.
3736 Eubank NE Suite A1
Albuquerque, NM 87111-3579
www.citiofbooks.com
Hotline: 1 (877) 389-2759
Fax: 1 (505) 930-7244

Ordering Information:
Quantity sales. Special discounts are available on quantity purchases by corporations, associations, and others. For details, contact the publisher at the address above.

Printed in the United States of America.

ISBN-13:   Softcover   979-8-89391-826-7
                  eBook   979-8-89391-827-4

Library of Congress Control Number: 2025915244

Dedicated to my very patient and very understanding wife
who has put up with me for the past forty-seven years

Prolog

Spiritual guidance governs all of us. Are our prayers always answered, yes but not in the way we expect. Can pre-ordained rule our lives or does man alone decide what destiny waits for himself and all mankind.

CHAPTER 1
July 2011 Thailand

It was a monster, huge with a tightly wound eye and outstretched arms causing massive amounts of destruction and death. It roared out of the South China Sea Tropical storm Noc-ten maleficent, winds exceeded over 100 mph causing waist high flooding. Thailand, having a low-level coastline, was in its path and could not escape the wrath of Typhoon Noc-ten that hit Thailand in July of 2011. The flooding was extensive, ruining the country's annual rice crops and other vital commodities. The death toll was enormous. Being a Buddhist nation there was no luxury or comfort during the 46-day mourning period for the dead.

For 15-year-old Cy Hing her family was spared but her wooden home, tin roof and farm animals were all gone. The family's rice paddies as she knew it were also destroyed by high flooding and terrible strong winds. Taking shelter, Cy Hing's mother and father and 3 younger siblings took shelter in the local schoolhouse as it was built on a small rising hill protecting them from only shallow flooding. The hollow brick building withstood the ferocious winds as well as three other families from their small village. With their rice crops ruined there would be nothing to sell in the Bangkok markets this year and probably the following year as well.

Other creatures did not fare as well either, a 6-foot-long fat Cobra washed out of its hole in the rice fields was disturbed at the disruption of its habitat. Fat and healthy from eating the rats that enjoyed gnawing the rice granules and plants, it was not hungry, just angry and agitated. It swam towards the schoolhouse as Cy Hing and her family waded through knee deep water to reach safety. Stealthy, silently swimming it swam towards the schoolhouse barely causing a wake as Cy Hing's family was focused on getting out of the water to safety. Without warning it struck at the legs of Cy Hing's mother. Screaming in horror at the site of the Cobra and the initial sting of its venom, the venom quickly coursed its way through her bloodstream, burning like a red-hot poker. With unbearable pain, her eyes bulging, gasping for air, her tongue protruding with heavy amounts of saliva drooling down her chin until the poison reached her heart and lungs. It was all over; she died a half hour later. Cy Hing's mother knew what her fate was going to be once she saw the fat cobra silently swimming; it did not even show any warning signs by flattening its neck and making its typical hood. Screaming in terror it would be just a matter of time before she went into labored breathing as the poisonous venom coursed its way through her body.

"Help me help me" she pleaded with her family and others who were in the schoolhouse but there was nothing anyone could do. A half hour later she was dead. Crying and grieving, her family watched as she slipped into darkness never to wake up again.

Cy Hing's father sat on a stool in the schoolhouse with a catatonic expression on his face not talking to anyone, he was lost, he did not know what to do or say. He covered her body with her sarong and laid her on the cement floor as respectfully as he could. His children realized for the first time in their lives their dire predicament as their family was facing the loss of their mother's home and land. Their youngest, a three-year-old boy, began wailing loudly, experiencing fright and no longer feeling the comfort and security of their home and the closeness of his family. Whatever Cy Hing did or said did not comfort him. Nighttime was fast approaching; it set very quickly like a sledgehammer in the tropics with there were no flashlights or food and only the annoying buzzing of mosquitoes in the humid and sticky air. For those that survived, the remaining three families of Cy Hing's small village had also taken refuge in the safety of the school, faced with the same situation and problems.

What were they to do?

"Talk to us Pappa, where will we live and what shall we eat, we've lost our dearly beloved mother, everything is gone"? said Cy Hing's crying hysterically. There was no answer, only the silence of a dark night. The dark night and the mocking gurgling of transient water still moved to consume whatever it touched. The wind had faded away by now, its work was already finished. Even the customary sounds of night animals and insects were absent. Clutching her small golden amulet of Buddha, she began praying as earnestly as she could.

"O blessed one Shakyamuni Buddha treasury of compassion,
Bestower of supreme inner peace,
You who love all things without exception,
Are the source of happiness and goodness.
And you guide us to the liberating path
Lord Buddha, please protect us and help our family
we need the generosity of your love and protection."

She kissed the small golden medallion that hung around her neck as she prayed to Buddha. It was the only icon available. Lord Buddha was swept away with all other iconic symbols of Buddhism. Cy Hing was deeply saddened, however, grateful for her remaining family that they were still alive. There were no sounds that night, just the quiet whimpering of terrified children. Cy Hing had read somewhere that the two greatest days in one's life are the day you were born and the day you realize why you were here. Was this my greatest day? The daylight illuminated the extent of the damage. The sun rises like it was shot out of a cannon instantaneously illuminating the disaster. The sight was dramatic, not a living soul, animal or bird could be seen, nothing but water. The water was lapping gently against the schoolhouse door. It was not receding; however, perhaps the early morning presented the promise of new events yet to come. The sun was shining brightly glaring off the flood waters sparkling diamonds, the air was calm and still.

Cy Hing heard it first a "put-put" motor sound from a wooden boat she had heard many times before as her father would take his annual rice crop to the miller in Bangkok. The boat contained two uniformed soldiers from the Thai army

"Hello! Is anyone there?" shouted a Thai soldier,

"Yes! We are here in the schoolhouse," shouted everyone. "Over here, over here, in the schoolhouse" they all said in unison.

"Our most beloved king has ordered the army to rescue as many people as possible who might still be alive, we cannot take any dead bodies." he said. "We will take you to a shelter for safety. It's operated by CARE International. They have shelter, food, water and medical supplies." one of the two soldiers said in a hopeful tone. "You can stay for several months until you decide what to do or where to go."

The four families walked down the small hill until they reached the water's edge where a long wooden boat and a long-motorized propeller jutted out 45 degrees away from the stern of the boat. It enabled the boat to travel easily in shallow waters. The two soldiers moored their boat as close as possible to enable the families to climb aboard. It was large enough to accommodate everyone but no room for the dead. The small group of survivors sat in gloom and silence with nothing but the clothes on their backs. They bowed in respect to Cy Hing's mother as they said their final tearful goodbyes. She was laid unceremoniously on the floor in the cement schoolhouse. Inevitably it became a mausoleum of sorts until finally her body was consumed by rats and other scavengers.

CHAPTER 2

Pyongyang, North Korea

Kim Jung Nam had become an embarrassment to his family. His father Kim Jun il the supreme leader of North Korea and his half-brother Kim Jung Un constantly argued and bickered with Kim Jung Nam about the situation in their country.

"I'm telling you! We must spend all the country's resources on defense, we must get military help from China and Russia as well. Who knows what will happen to us if the south and the American allies decide to invade us, we must have artillery, rifles, ammunition, planes, bombs and even missiles and rockets to defend ourselves" said Kim Jung Il to his two children with as much earnestness as he could muster.

"But father," said Kim Jung Nam "what about our people?" They are starving, bad weather and drought have destroyed crops this year. there is not enough to eat, there is not enough food to go around. Our people are starving. We need to reach out to help them. They need housing, education, and a stable supply of food."

"The hell with the people '' said Kim Jun Un, "let them die they will be dead anyway if the Americans and the South overrun our country" Kim Jung Un muttered in a matter-of-fact tone. "Our people do not need education, and they should be able to. grow their food without governmental assistance, let them fend for themselves. We need to defend ourselves first. Kim Jung Un'' said emphatically.

"I have sent a letter to our defense minister and our war council asking for their advice. They all replied to my request and replied that we should focus as much as possible on our country's defense and borrow as much as possible from China and Russia and so I have decided to focus on defense and less on our people. We must give the impression that we have a strong military and not to be trifled with. We will educate our people to love us with movies glorifying ourselves, giant posters of our supreme leaders as the people's father figures and huge military parades glorifying our country's military's strength. They will soon forget about the misery of their lives and they will learn to love us despite their misery. They will learn to address me as our dear leader and look at me as a father figure" said Kim Jun Il with finality.

The quarrel and bickering went on for several years. Eventually, Kim Jung Nam began disclosing sensitive information to western newspapers and interviews with neighboring countries regarding the plight of the North Korean people. Despite heavy censorship, it was embarrassing to Kim Jung Il and Kim Jung Un, they realized he needed to be silenced but in such a way that would be done covertly without the people knowing about it, he was family.

In 2003, Kim Jung Nam was brought before the Supreme Council with the charges of seditious and treasonable activities against the Government of North Korea. He was found guilty, but luckily not executed. North Korean justice can be quite brutal and harsh with no recourse for appeals or forgiveness. As a result, his punishment for Kim Jung Nam was banishment for life from North Korea. So, in 2003 he was exiled never to come back home. However, during his lifetime in North Korea, he had silently managed to surreptitiously squirrel away a hefty sum of money-making deposits into the Bank of BBL Pharate in Bangkok Thailand. Not even his half-brother knew about the secret deposits.

It had been two months since the deadly typhoon came ashore in Thailand. Cy Hing and her family were still living at the CARE International camp in Bangkok It was midday, and the sun was brutally hot. There had been no rain for six weeks making for long hot days. Cy Hing decided to take her mid-day shower at the outdoor community well. Bringing her towel, bucket and a long rope while wearing only her sarong that covered her breasts to her knees. Lowering her bucket, she drew the water from the well and poured the water over herself, refreshing her hot sticky body. Her wet sarong clung tightly to her body revealing her shape from her petite breasts and nipples down to the outline of her pubic area. Her shoulders and beautiful brown skin glistened in the sunlight. Her long black hair that hung down to her waist and smoothness of her shoulders radiated natural beauty and subtle sensuality. She was not aware how beautiful she looked.

However, her looks did not go unnoticed, Fu Lei the owner of several hotels in Bangkok caught his eye. Fu Lei was making his rounds looking for young girls to work in his hotels. Thinking to himself, "European Men would like a woman like that" after seeing Cy Hing take her mid-day outdoor shower. European Men enjoyed looking for small petite looking young Asian women when they came to Bangkok for their holidays, they would pay a lot of money to spend a night with a woman like Cy Hing he thought to himself. European Men were looking to get away from overweight, chain smoking, spend happy, overbearing European Women.

"No! I will not!" she screamed out loudly.

"You must! You must!" he said emphatically.

"No! I refuse to go" she burst out screaming and crying hysterically at the same time. "I cannot and will not go!" screaming as loudly as she could.

"You have to, you have no choice in the matter" I have made up my mind."

"Please! Please! Please! Do not do this." she said, while lying prostrate at his feet begging her father to change his mind.

"It is done, I have sold you to Mr. Fu Lei, '' said Cy Hing's father. "He will pay me 100,000 Bhat (approximately $2600). With the money from your sale, I can reclaim my land and restart my rice fields. I will be able to feed your younger brothers. You have no mother, and I have three small children to look after. How will I ever do that without any money? Think about your siblings, your sacrifice will give our family honor. At least we can get out of this stinking camp."

Cy Hing lay at his feet crying while prostrate on the floor. She did not expect her father to sacrifice her as a prostitute and work in the Bangkok sex industry. So, for the sake of her family, she acquiesced to the realization of working in the sex industry. The very next day she accompanied Mr. Fu Lei along with a bag containing all her worldly belongings and proceeded to her place of one of Mr. Fu Lei's hotels. Mr. Fu Lei was a balding diminutive man wearing only a white sleeveless tank top and khaki shorts but had access to money that bought him political and social power.

Thailand's constitution forbids prostitution and is against the law, but it is such a lucrative business that the sex entrepreneurs and government both share equally in the royalties originating from the sex trade. Even married women with children will pursue a trade in prostitution as it is a means of providing a steady income for their families. Thailand government has turned its back on the trade and looks at it with a blind eye. Cy Hing was one of many of the 150,000 Thai sex workers that attract mostly male tourists from all over the world.

CHAPTER 3
Leipzig Germany

2015

Heinrich Baldinger was a junior accountant at one of the many industrial coal mines surrounding Leipzig, a German industrial city not too far from the German North Coast. He was in his late thirties, overweight with his hair growing on one side of his head. He would comb it over to cover his entire scalp, but it would look like strands of spaghetti just laying on top of his bald head. Heinrich had let himself go after his marriage, corpulent and selfish he lived a mundane life. His wife was no better looking, a chain-smoker with a large rotund bottom so that her appearance took on the shape of a bowling pin. She was quite satisfied to spend her husband's paycheck and gossip with her girlfriends at the local beauty parlor once a month. She had no interest in her husband's activities. They had no children. She also had limited interest in sex with her husband. Heinrich sometimes got lucky as she allowed him to have sex with her once every 6 months. Their marriage was one of convenience for economic and social situation without any unrequited love. Heinrich had told his wife that his only hobby is fishing and that he belongs to a local fishing club in Leipzig. He told his wife that once a year he and his club will go on a fishing destination of their choosing, in Russia or the Mediterranean. She could not care less where he went, she had no interest in her husband's life On one occasion, he saw a travel poster, advertising the natural wonders of Thailand: "The sandy beaches, the warm clear ocean and a privately escorted female guide to show you all the exotic places Thailand has to offer." And of course, Heinrich noticed it right away.

Occasionally, Cy Hing would ask Mr. Fu Lei for her wages that she had earned as a prostitute; however, he would only give her money for her personal needs. It prevented her from buying a train or plane ticket so she could run away from her desperate plight.

"I'll save your money, and only give you what you need. Then one day when you really need it, I'll give you all of it. But in the meantime, let me keep it in a safe place so that none of those European tourists might steal your money. Of course, he had no intention of ever giving Cy Hing her money. She hated being a sex worker. It was demeaning and disgusting, three times she had run away and three times she was found, not having enough money to travel very far. She was severely beaten by Mr. Fu Lei each time she ran away. She simply did not have the money to get very far from the sex industry in Bangkok.

So, in 2015 Heinrich Ballinger made his annual pilgrimage to Thailand to spend as many nights as he could with as many different Thai ladies. he could afford.

It was his last night in Bangkok before returning to Germany. To celebrate his last night in Bangkok he decided to get drunk. Heinrich had put away at least six bottles of beer before the hotel manager Mr. Fu Lei brought Cy Hing to his room. Paying his customary fee to Mr. Fu Lei and not Cy Hing. Heinrich was delighted as to what he saw; she looked exotic and sensual. There was no talking as neither one knew the other's language, but she knew what was expected of her, and silently took off her clothes and crawled into Heinrich's hotel bed, patiently waiting for him to undress. In the meantime, Heinrich finished another beer and began undressing. He mimed to Cy Hing to get on all fours on top of the bed with her head pointing to the headboard and her feet pointing to the base board. Heinrich took off his belt and forced it into her mouth like reins on a horse, he straddled her back while thrusting a bottle of opened beer into her rectum. She screamed in pain and agony as he tore through her anus and into her descending colon and vagina. Squealing in pain she could not move under the corpulent weight of Heinrich's body. Taking both ends of his belt he began riding Cy Hing as though she was a horse, at the same time masturbating on top of her back. At the time of his ejaculation, he violently pulled out the open bottle of beer from her rectum. Out came a torrent of fluids: beer, blood, and feces. She screamed in agonizing pain. His semen squirted on the back of her neck and slowly dribbled into her eyes and mouth. Heinrich had fulfilled a fantasy that his wife would never give him. Yes, there were sex workers in Germany, but they were never like these petite young Thai ladies with their smooth brown skin, petite breasts, and soft long black hair. He slowly sloughed off Cy Hing's back, rolled onto his side and fell fast asleep in a drunken stupor. For Heinrich he fulfilled a fantasy. He knew his wife would never know what he did on his annual fishing trips. For Cy Hing she was in burning pain she could barely walk, profusely bleeding from her perineum from her anus to her vagina. She found her clothing and dressed herself. Barely walking, she eventually packed her underwear with tampons to address the bleeding, she stood there looking at Heinrich. Fat, balding, snoring like a pig and with an equally disgusting view of sex. Content to lie there without a care in the world, not even gratitude to Cy Hing for fulfilling his fantasy. "Buddha where are you?" She held her amulet of Buddha:

Lord buddha please here my prayer
Let my heart turn to practice.
Let practice become a become a path.
Let this path dissolve confusion.
Let confusion become wisdom.

'Why is it that I must be a slave of these fat balding disgusting men? Why must they brutally abuse and control me" Cy Hing said to herself. She was not alone. Even in the most democratic of countries fat balding old men continue to control the fates of women.

Still looking at Heinrich she saw his wallet bulging out of his back pocket as his pants lay on the floor. She took it and saw there were about 2,000 Bhat. "I will take all of his money, ' she said to herself. It was enough to buy a train ticket to get as far away from Bangkok as possible. Mr. Fu Lei would never be able to find me. But first, she needed to get to a hospital as quickly as possible. Her doctor at the emergency clinic sewed and sutured her perineum. He had never seen any abuse bad as this to a sex worker in Bangkok.

"Please don't tell the owner of the hotel where I am." she pleaded with the doctor.

"Don't worry Cy Hing your secret is good with me, but you need to get out of the sex business before it kills you", he said in a sympathetic voice.

"One day I will become someone important who can stop the trade of selling young girls into prostitution. I will never do this again." she said to the sympathetic doctor. She paid the doctor for his services with the money she had stolen from Heinrich Baldinger. Feeling better after taking her pain pills and antibiotics, she proceeded to the railway station and bought a ticket as far as she could go and still had some money left over for living expenses. Eight hours later she arrived at the city of Chiang Mai. Heinrich was left without any money and a missing plane ticket with no ID Cy Hing took everything. He would have to come up with a better excuse for his wife other than "gone fishing!"

Chiang Mai is famous for its water festival. It is an annual event marking the start of the traditional Thai new year. It is the one day when anyone can throw, spray, toss, splash, squirt water on anyone anywhere, anytime without anyone getting angry at getting drenched with water. It is expected it usually was extremely hot at this time of year, the water felt very cool and refreshing. It did not matter if you were a Buddhist priest, or a European or Australian tourists it was expected you were to get wet. Chiang Mai became packed with tourists and locals and the crowded streets. She came to the first restaurant she saw as she walked away from the train station.

"Excuse me madam," said Cy Hing shyly. Do you need any help in your restaurant?"

"What is your name child?"

"My name is Cy Hing, and I need work and a place to stay, can you help me please?"

"Ah, your name means princess," said Mrs. Ananya. "Can you cook? With all these hungry tourists around I need someone to work my outside stall. I don't have enough cooks to keep up with these hungry tourists."

" Cy Hing recognized a possible solution to her problem

"Noodles, curry, rice, fish, vegetables. You name it I can do it. I used to do it for my family" she said.

"So why aren't you cooking for your family anymore?"

"It's a long story, Mrs. Ananya. I just can't talk about it right now, "she said with tight lips.

Mrs. Ananya recognized the hidden pain on Cy Hing's face.

"Ok then here is my offer, I need help badly, I will pay you steady wages, you can keep your tips if any. Americans like to tip, and you can sleep in my restaurant. There is something I like about you." spoke. Mrs. Ananya. "You can start tomorrow." she said firmly.

Finally, Cy Hing felt the throbbing pain in her perineum subside, so she was able to relax and feel better about herself. "Surely Mr. Fu Lei will never find me here and thank you Buddha for showing me my hidden path and the day of my beginning" she closed her eyes and went to sleep.

Over the months Cy Hing did well with her cooking, she earned some notoriety to the locals who came to enjoy her dishes at Mrs. Ananya's restaurant. In time she slowly revealed her history to Mrs. Ananya: the typhoon, losing her family's land, the cobra killing her mother, her father selling her into prostitution, the beatings from Mr. Fu Lei, the abuse and assault she received from that German Tourist. Mrs. Ananya recognized that Cy Hing was a special and brave young lady. She was glad to have her working at her restaurant.

1975 saw the Thai new year roll in again, and once again Cheng Mai was crowded with tourists for the annual celebratory water festival. Stepping off the train was Mr. Fu Lei carrying a long bamboo cane. Walking quickly, he headed to Mrs. Ananya's restaurant. Sy Hing saw him coming and froze in fear.

"So! You think you can hide here in Cheng Mai. Don't you know I was born and raised in this town? It was only a matter of time before my friends and family told me you were here. Now I've found you again, you will come back with me. I own you" he said with maliciousness in his voice. And with his long cane he began whipping Sy Hing, slashing her on her shoulders, tearing her skin in long wide gashes, in public in front of everyone at Mrs. Ananya's restaurant. Cy Hing pleaded for mercy as she screamed for help. Before he could strike her again, a customer eating at Mrs. Ananya's restaurant, grabbed Mr. Fu Lei's hand, stopping him in midair before he could whip Cy Hing even more. Seizing a nearby frying pan from the outside stove he struck Mr. Fu Lei's head three times with it knocking him seriously unconscious.

"Thank you, sir," she said, bleeding and trembling at being flogged with a bamboo cane.

"Not to worry, my name is Kim Jong Nam. I hate to see a defenseless woman being abused. I have seen enough of that in my own country. I am Korean and I've been living in Thailand for 10 years now. I can speak your language, and I have knowledge of your Buddhist customs and beliefs. You will be OK now" he said softly and politely. When the Thai police arrived, there were no arrests as everyone spoke on behalf of the stranger how the stranger came to the aid of this poor defenseless girl from being whipped for no apparent reason. Mr. Fu Lei was taken to a local hospital for his battered head. His concussion was so severe that he never recovered his speech and ambulatory skills. He was resigned to sitting in a wheelchair without speech for the rest of his life.

Mrs. Ananya asked the stranger to stay for a nice meal courtesy of the house and to have Cy Hing sit at the table. With her wounds dressed and finally free of Mr. Fu Lei the three of them sat at the table eating a fabulous meal while he began telling his story.

"After my banishment from Korea I had nowhere to go. Since my money was kept at a bank in Bangkok, I decided to make Thailand my home. I have traveled all over your country from Sungai Golok in the south to Phuket Island in the west, all the time learning your language and customs. I decided that I should come to Cheng Mail to see your legendary water festival, and I heard your dishes are wonderful, Mrs. Ananya," while looking at Cy Hing. With deliberate thought he asked Cy Hing if he could see her again. He also recognized her bravery and beauty. She was caught off guard as men only asked her for sex, never for social contact. Clearly uncomfortable, she agreed that he could see her.

Every day for a month Kim Jong Nam came to the restaurant to see Cy Hing, until she was at ease with him and enjoyed his visits. She also explained her background and how she arrived at Cheng Mai. It did not faze him, only respected her more. Until one day he asked Cy Hing a peculiar question.

"Cy Hing I will be leaving for Bangkok soon; I want you to come with me as my paramour and companion. I have enough money for both of us and my work is not done against my half-brother. I want you to help me and advise me. You are free to come and go as you please, there are no restrictions on you.", the thought of leaving intrigued her but she did not want to leave Mrs. Ananya.

"My child, your life is in Buddha's hands, listen to your heart. Never mind about me. I will always be here if you need me" she said with sadness in her eyes.

There was something about Kim Jung Nam; appealed to her; she was attracted to his caring and gentle manners as so was allured to his way of life. She had never known the gentleness of a man; she began to enjoy their love for him and wanted to be his companion wherever he went and what he did.

Several weeks later Cy Hing and Kim Jong Nam took the train to Bangkok to start their campaign against his half-brother. During the time in Bangkok, he revealed to her all of North Korea's classified vital secrets that the West never knew.

"Did you know that a Chinese delegation came to Pyongyang to talk to his half-brother?" He said cautiously to Cy Hing.

"Why? she replied.

"Listen carefully, I have never told this to anyone. A Chinese delegation of the highest priority came to see Kim Jong Un about a deal with China. They persuaded my half-brother to begin building rockets and missiles and develop possible nuclear capabilities. China would supply all the resources including financing and fissionable materials to my country.

"In exchange for what?" she asked curiously.

"China wants to build offshore islands in the South China Sea. They want to develop artificial offshore islands for economic and military reasons. By having Chinese controlled islands in international waters, they can force shipping to pay tax shipping duties the way Hong Kong and Singapore do and have a base for military and naval preparedness for eventual attacks against Taiwan. By doing this they would have complete control of commerce, military, and naval bases in the South China Sea.

"Why the rockets and missiles?" she asked.

"Because if the West and neighboring Southeast Asian countries became fully aware about the development of secret artificial islands that China is building in the South China Sea, then China would receive a tremendous amount of international criticism and trade sanctions from all sides of the world. So, if my half-brother could begin firing long range ICBM missiles over Japan. The focus of the world would be on criticizing North Korea for its development of missiles with nuclear warheads and long-range missiles. By doing this it would take China out of the spotlight for its efforts to clandestinely build artificial islands. So that, China could build its artificial islands with little condemnation from the global community. It would be a smoke screen for China to quietly build their offshore islands while the world's eyes are looking at North Korea.

"Does your half-brother plan on using them to hit Japan, Wake Island and Alaska or Hawaii?" she said in a frightened tone.

"No it is only a bluff only to scare the west and neighboring countries in Southeast Asia to make believe he would do it. Kim Jong Un knows what the ramifications would be if he did it. In the meantime, he will keep on firing missiles provoking the west and Japan's attention on North Korea as China continues to build its offshore islands under the smoke screen of Kim Jon Un's faux military exercises.

"So did the Chinese government begin building their secret offshore islands."

"So far, I believe they have built three of them and I think they are going to start a new artificial island 15 miles off the coast of Malaysia. I also know there will be more plans for nine more islands like a string of pearls to be built somewhere in the South China Sea. It allows China to have a platform to blockade Taiwan's microchip trade and have a naval and air platform to launch attacks anywhere along the South China Sea. I don't know how, but it will be done hastily and as clandestinely and covertly as possible as long as my country continues to fire missiles over Japan. It allows my country to deflect World criticism to be focused on my country and not on China. Somehow they will be built, anywhere in shallow waters close to Taiwan, Malaysia, Vietnam or even the Philippines. China could control world trade as the world shipping lanes for commerce similarly traveling through the Straits of Malacca or Singapore or even Hong Kong, now global shipping would have to pass by those Chinese artificial islands and China could demand royalties from the shipping companies and a military platform for eventual military attacks.

"Cy Hing, listen to me closely! Please do not share this information with anyone, it will endanger your life and mine. My contacts in North Korea are slowly revealing this information to me. Until I am ready to tell the western newspapers, you must keep this a secret, tell no one your life would be in danger", he said emphatically."

Here is a document written in English, make your way to any American Embassy, in case you are in danger. Hide it well use it when you must, hopefully it will save your life one day, do you understand." "Yes, but what does it say?"

"My name is Cy Hing, I am a citizen of Thailand, North Korean agents are trying to kill me. I have vital information regarding North Korea's nuclear rocket and missile programs, I wish to share what I know with the west. I am seeking asylum in America." She tucked the note down into her bra, it was the only safe place she could think would work at the time. In the time she and Kim Jung Nam were together he told her many secret and sensitive North Korean secrets including access to his bank account in Bangkok.

CHAPTER 4

Fort Rucker Army Helicopter
Training Base, Alabama

2016

"Colonel Garron I am Cam Hayes's son my name is Captain Ali Razak bin Hayes as he reported for duty at Fort Rucker

" Yes, I have been expecting you, Captain Hayes. So, you are Cam Hayes's son I'll be damned. He was my co-pilot. We did three missions in Beirut and Malaysia together twenty odd years or ago. He resigned from the Army and married your mother I believe."

"That is true sir, my father told me all about you, he said you were the best helicopter pilot he had ever flown with, that is why I am here sir to learn from the best. My government sought to do that and made special arrangements with your government to learn how to fly those top-secret helicopters at Fort Rucker's flight school."

"So, tell me how is ole Cam these days? We don't write much anymore."

"Quite well actually my parents opened a hotel on the beach and franchised it with Club Med, it is quite popular with the Japanese tourists. As my father predicted that our government would eventually deliver electricity and running water to the area, he was right."

21

"We have made room for you in the officer's barracks. You will then start training you how to fly our super-duper fancy helicopters of ours along with a co-pilot." said.

Colonel Garron"

"I can't wait to get started sir."

Ali Razak bin Hayes was born in Malaysia after his father converted to Islam at the end of his tour of enlistment of his tour of duty from the US Army, he decided to stay in Malaysia to marry a Malay Woman. His conversion to Islam from Christianity was not too difficult, however his circumcision and the prohibition to drink beer or eating pork provided some tense moments but he was able to manage his difficulties. Ali Razak bin Hayes was the youngest of three children, a Muslim, he decided he would follow his father's footsteps. True to his father's background he received a Malaysian scholarship to receive his bachelor's degree from Stanford University. Returning home, Ali Razak entered the military as a flying officer and began learning how to fly helicopters. Being the best in his class, Ali Razak was picked to be assigned to Fort Rucker to learn how to fly the US Army's most advanced tactical helicopter. It was a top-secret mission…

Colonel Jackson reflected for a moment on his last mission 20 years ago with the US Army and Cam Hayes.

…Cam Hayes, two Lieutenants and a squad of Malaysian Rangers flew into mainland Thailand to eliminate a Chinese Communist stronghold that was terrorizing Malaysia. Unknowingly flying into an ambush, the communists were well prepared to repel the surprise attack. During the foray Jackson received third degree burns on both hands trying to rescue a Malaysian officer who was tangled up in his safety harness while his craft was still burning Cam Hayes lost part of his vision from an exploding RPG round that exploded in front of his craft shattering his windshield forcing debris into Cam's eyes. Both were eventually rescued, Jackson was sent to the Philippines to a Mobile Army Surgical Hospital burn unit, it was there he found Mena Delacruz, a nurse he had once known in Beirut. Cam Hayes was sent to the Army Hospital in Honolulu to repair his damaged eyesight. It was there in Honolulu that he decided to give up his commission and go back to Malaysia to marry a Muslim woman he had fallen in love with…

Jackson Garron stayed in the Army after marrying Mena Dela Cruz an Army nurse assigned to the Philippines. Jackson was promoted to captain and sent to Fort Rucker as a flight instructor, Cam Hayes opened a hotel on the beach on the East Coast of Malaysia. And now after 20 years, here in my office, comes Cam Hayes's son, captain Ali Razak bin Hayes of the Malaysian Army.

"It's funny how things work out. What's that saying what goes around comes around? Those Hindu beliefs about reincarnation has a lot to say for it self," he thought to himself.

It took Ali Razak bin Hayes after nine months of flying time to learn how to fly specialized helicopters. Coming off the production line in Area 51 Nevada the experimental Apache helicopter was outfitted with a specialized designed exterior armored plated skin that deflected radar waves and made it invisible on radar even at slow speeds. It was often mistaken for UFO's as it was flown only at night.

CHAPTER 5

Pyongyang Korea

2016

"Why is that bastard half-brother of mine telling everyone what is going on in my own country?" Kim Jong Un said to his war minister. "This has to stop! I'm tired of all these stories appearing in newspapers around the world about the famine in North Korea. There is no famine, our people are happy and love us. They are well fed and very prosperous" Despite evidence from The World Health Organization showing that millions of North Koreans are starving for food in North Korea and are living at a subsistence level.

"Don't you know anyone that could put an end to all this?" he said with an underlying tone in his voice.

"We will see what we can do" replied the war minister in an acknowledging tone.

Korean agents know where to go to find clandestine agents to do their dirty work for them.

Money is a strong motivator it allows potential assassins from poverty stricken South East Asian Countries to despite risking their lives for money. Two women, one from Vietnam and one from Indonesia eagerly accepted the proposition to assassinate Kim Jung Nam. Even Korea has access to computers and track international passenger lists and passport numbers. Kim Jong Nam's name showed up on their passenger manifest list revealing that Kim Jong Nam accompanied by a Thai female had booked a flight to Malaysia to be an honorary guest speaker at the University of Malaya's' political science department. However, at the last moment they canceled their appearance at the University of Malaya and rebooked a flight to Macau. Kim Jong Nam sensed that this trip to Malaysia did not feel right, it may mean trouble for him and Cy Hing. At the last moment he and Cy Hing felt better about spontaneously going to Macau instead of the University of Malaya. Close to boarding two ladies crept up behind Kim Jong Nam and covered his face with a towel that was saturated with VX, a highly poisonous deadly nerve gas. Gagging and covering his mouth and nose he could not breathe. He vomited and thrashed violently like a snake with its head cut off. But the two assassins held on tightly to Kim Jung Nam's body. Aspirating into his own lungs he drowned from his own vomit. To the astonished airline passengers, they did not know what to do or what was happening. In 15 minutes, Kim Jung Nam was dead. Cy Hing, not knowing what to do, ran for her life as she thought she might be next. Siti Aishia from Indonesia and Doan Thi Huang from Vietnam were paid very handsomely for their service to the government of Kim Jong Un. Airport security cameras were able to reveal and identify the two assassins. It did not take much time for Malaysian Security Forces to capture the two assassins Doan Thi Huang was found guilty and sentenced to three years in jail. Siti Aishia was found innocent and let go. They were both willing to accept Malaysian punishment metered out from the Malaysian Justice system; it did not bother the two assassins; it was worth the money they received. Kim Jung Nam was dead, and Cy Hing was nowhere to be found.

CHAPTER 6

Pyongyang North Korea

February 2017

The Chinese delegation to Pyongyang was incredibly angry at Kim Jong Un as they met at his presidential palace.

"Why haven't you shot more missiles over Japan?" said an angry Bingwen Chin leader of the Chinese delegation to Kim Jung Un's embarrassed moon face. "We have given you everything you need to develop your missile program and nuclear programs, yet you are not shooting enough missiles over Japan. Why are you so slow?"

"It's because of this American President Trump. He wants to be my friend, and he sends letters to me. He even said he loves me. Can you imagine that! His aides are reaching out to us making overtures that President Trump is wanting to eventually have a meeting with me at the DMZ sometime next year. What should I do? World opinion wants us to meet to resolve our differences. Already we are receiving world criticism for firing too many missiles over Japan."

"That is fine, it still focuses world opinion on your country and not on ours. We are out of the spotlight. Until we have finished our mission building our artificial islands" said Bingwen Chin in a lighter mood.

"If you do not shoot more missiles towards Japan then we will cut off all aid to North Korea, already your people are starving, and your infrastructure is very frail. You'll need our help badly, other than Russia or maybe Iran, no one else will help you. We don't care what you do with President Trump, do what you must to look good, but we want you to fire more missiles over Japan. We need you to receive world criticism to be focused on North Korea so we can conduct our secret programs and divert world criticism towards you. We can then continue with our artificial island program without receiving notice from the United Nations. Already the Philippines, Malaysia, South Vietnam, and Australia are beginning to complain to the US and the UN of the three islands we have built. We want a smokescreen so that we can build our artificial islands in the South China Seas. We want North Korea in the spotlight so that we can stay in the dark. Do you understand?" Bingwen Chin emphatically said.Kim Jung Un said he understood he did not wish to lose his country's only benefactor. However, he was satisfied that his half-brother was no longer in the picture and no longer a threat to his power by sharing state secrets with journalists and other countries.

CHAPTER 7

Langley Virginia, CIA Headquarters

March 1ˢᵗ, 2017

"Who in the hell is that woman?" said Bruce Chan, Deputy Assistant Secretary for the US State Department while looking at the airports' closed-circuit tape of Kim Jung Nam's murder.

"We just got the tape of Kim Jung Nam's assassination." his aide said. "However, the Malaysian Security Forces knew who the hell she is since they have her passport and identification papers. They knew who she is but will not share that information with us. However, they did send the tape to us as a courtesy."

"Well, who is she?" he asked again impatiently.

"Well sir, we just do not know who she is. The Malaysian Government refuses to tell us for their national security reasons. They will not release her background to us until they want a private meeting with us in KL. Only then will they share any information with us."

"Why, and what kind of meeting?" Bruce said.

"We don't know," his aide said "they want a private tete-a- tete with us. There is something in the air we do not know about." his aide said with quiet resolution.,

"OK then, get this tape over to the National Security boys, they can figure it out, who in the hell is this woman? We had better find out before we have our meeting in KL. Who is our best man in KL?"

28

Kim Jung Nan had an uneasy sense about coming to Malaysia, he wanted a backup plan in case something dramatic happened to him and Cy Hing.

"Listen Cy Hing in case something goes wrong, and you can't rebook your flight to Macau. After running and hiding for so long I've learned how to sense danger. If something goes wrong while we are in Kuala Lumpur hail a taxi just say, Hotel Lido in Brickfields." The owner of the hotel is an Indian chap, his name is Hardeep Singh. He is a friend of mine from a long time ago. We met in Phuket Island in your country. For your safety write down Hotel Lido Brickfields on that piece of paper I gave you earlier.

Cy Hing ran out of the airport after the assassination of Kim Jung Nam. She raised her hand signaling a taxi. She spoke to the taxi driver as Kim Jung Nam had instructed. "Hotel Lido Brickfields," she said in a hurried breath.

On arrival at the Hotel Lido, Cy Hing showed Mr. Singh the note she had safeguarded with her life.

"Ah you must be Kim Jung Nam's friend," Hardeep Singh, manager of The Hotel Lido said in a surprised tone. "He called me and said you might be coming and perhaps you might be in trouble,"

She nodded her head as though she understood.

The hotel Lido has two equal courtyards, facing each other. The hotel had three stories. Each story had its own balcony. The cement balconies were lined with the days of washing clothes draped from one end to the other to dry in the hot sun, each floor was crowded for space for the laundry to dry. In the front of the hotel was an outdoor restaurant specializing in Roti Chanai (rice pancake and chicken curry and Tay Tarik.

(tea being poured from one glass to another often-called flying tea) the two structures faced inward forming a roman numeral two. Between each structure ran a central open aired concrete sewage drain which enabled rats to run back and forth as freely as they wish. This was not a luxury hotel like Kuala Lumpur is famous for. This was a bare boned, no-frills hotel, with a single bed, one sheet, a tap for running water and a plastic bowl for washing your hands after feces elimination (there is no toilet paper) and a hole through the concrete floor for urine and feces elimination. With one dimly lit light centered between the blades of a squeaky fan provided all the illumination and cooling each guest would need.

She spent a restless night unsure what each day would bring and how she could get back to Thailand. She was alone, a stranger in this Muslim country. The loss of Kim Jung Nam was mind numbing. She had learned to love him but always allowed Kim Jung Nam to make decisions for both. There was a sharp rap on her door!

While having his morning coffee and cigarette the taxicab driver read the morning news in the New Strait Times, the Malaysian English written newspaper. The front page described the murder of Kim Jung Nam. It also described the mysterious woman who fled the scene at the time of Kim Jung Nam's murder. There would be a small reward of Ringgits MR 5, OOO It did not take much time to drive to Security headquarters.

"I know where she is" he blurted out at the duty officer's desk.

"Where who is?" annoyed while being interrupted with his paperwork."

"The girl from the airport she's in the news" the cab driver responded eagerly.

"Well why didn't you say so? I am sitting here doing paperwork and you know where this fugitive is. Let's go! Shouting as loudly as possible. Malaysian Security Forces were still in possession of her passport and her identity card when Cy Hing had checked through airport security.

CY Hing timidly opened the door and went to the front of the hotel, not knowing Bahasa Malaysia or English she stood there in fear like a statue frozen in front of the hotel. Another officer slapped handcuffs on her and led her out of the room to the awaiting Black Mariah. (Moniker left over from the British Colonial days for a paddy wagon)

Possession of her passport and her identity card revealed when Cy Hing had checked through airport security were retained by Malaysian Security.

"We'll let you know once we have her" he said to the taxi driver as he ran out of the door with two other junior officers and four cadres.

"How dangerous can a lone woman be" while smiling to himself as a potential promotion may be in the offering as he explained to the other members of his detail what had just transpired.

"Malaysian Security Forces! Come out now!" shouted an officer from the security detail using a loud and blaring bull horn.

"I know where she is he shouted one more time, I can show you, she showed me a note saying Hotel Lido. He shouted urgently. So, I took her there and she paid me well. When do I get my MR5,000 Ringgits? "He repeated hopefully.

"You will have to file some paperwork before you get your money. Once she is adjudicated then you can have the reward money. However, the officer in charge conveniently planned to lose the taxi driver's paperwork.

"We'll let you know once we have her" as he ran out of the door with two other junior officers and four cadre "

"Cy Hing, come out! Cy Hing came out and stood in the lobby of the hotel. This is the Malaysian Security Forces as he arrived and his cadre at the front of the Hotel Lido." The bull horn was loud and harsh as the officer in charge sounded out her name in English. She neither knew English or Bahasa Malaysia but she distinctly heard her name which meant she knew that Malaysian Security Forces knew of her whereabouts and her identity. Timidly, she exited the lobby and went to the front of the hotel leaving all her belongings behind. She was immediately handcuffed and taken away in the Black Mariah.

Washington DC

"Who in the hell is that woman?" said Bruce Chan repeated Deputy Assistant Secretary for the US State Department while looking at the airports' closed-circuit tape of Kim Jung Nam's murder.

"OK then, get this tape over to the National Security boys, maybe they can figure it out, who in the hell is this woman. We had better find out before we have our meeting in KL. Who is our man in KL?"

"His name is Trenton Winchester, he is a good man, ex-military, ex Peace Corp skilled in Bahasa Malaysia, and Thai. He received his master's from Naval Post Graduate school in Monterey. His major was Southeast Asian languages He is stationed in KL as an agricultural information officer to the Malaysian Government" said Bruce Chan's aide proudly.

"Good get him up to speed and set up a meeting in KL with us," Bruce said excitedly. "We got to know who this woman is."

Kuala Lumpur

She spent a restless night in a locked security area, unsure what each day would bring and how could she get back to Thailand? She was alone, a stranger in this Muslim country. The loss of Kim Jung Nam was mind numbing. She had learned to love him but always allowed Kim Jung Nam to make decisions for both. He told her many things about North Korea's secrets There was a sharp rap on her door!

CHAPTER 8

Area 51 Nevada

2018

Deep in a top-secret hangar in Area 51 Nevada, Captain Hayes and Colonel Garron were discussing and looking at a top-secret bomb that had never been used before.

"Do you think this thing will work?" said to Captain Hayes to

Jackson Garron from the US Army elite operations flight team.

"It's got to, we have experimented with this thing in the lab and have done hypothetical tests and everything looks great and even have done dummy runs with smaller bombs, so far all looks good."

"Why does the nose have a corkscrew shape?" said Captain Hayes?"

"I've never seen a bomb as large as this and shaped like a corkscrew, and I'm not sure if my craft can even carry it to the IP.

"We call it the "Tire- Bouchon" which means corkscrew in French; one of our NATO allies, the French, proposed the idea to us several years ago. Yes, Captain Hayes the bomb weighs five thousand tons, 20 feet long 6 ft in diameter. It carries almost one thousand tons of ultra-high energy explosives. It is designed to burrow underground to about

1,000 feet deep into the earth. The nose cone of the bomb has an electric motor designed to burrow into the Earth. That's why it has a corkscrewed shape nose cone driven by al electric motor, at the precise depth it'll explode deep underground providing a signal simulating a seaquake or undersea earthquake. We have used heavy 3,000-ton bunker buster bombs in Afghanistan to blow up underground bunkers with enormous success but burrowing only about 20 feet underground to hit military underground bunkers."

"Why not use laser nuclear bunker bombs, they are quite effective."

"Correct Captain, however nuclear guided bunker bombs leave too much evidence such as where it came from and who made it. Very soon on this mission, we are sending you to Malaysia on a top-secret mission. Hopefully it will leave no trace evidence who made it and who dropped it Tomorrow we are going to load the "Tire- Bouchon" bomb onto an ultra-modified helicopter your dad and I flew in Beirut, Thailand, and Malaysia twenty years ago. We plan to drop the bomb on a test site on federal land close to Ridgecrest California, a small town out in the California desert with a population of 27,000 people. There is a naval air station there at China Lake where we can manufacture "tire-Bouchon"- we can use it without harming any civilian structures or destroying the environment. We will set the timing fuse for 500 feet underground and at that depth an explosion will happen. If the boys at Caltech are still monitoring their seismic instruments, they should see a reading of about 6.5 on the Richter Scale, located on the eastern part of California. There was also a small tsunami that traveled up and down the West Coat and even on to Hawaii. The good news is there was no damage to our coastline and to Hawaii as well."

"Inshallah (God willing) Colonel, why are you picking me for this mission?" Captain Hussein said in astonishment.

"I will explain to you later once the test was affirmative. We will have a briefing with you and your copilot when we are ready "

On July 4th, 2019, an earthquake occurred near the town of Ridgecrest in California with aftershocks on July 5th. Captain Hayes received a 4pm phone call from colonel Garran.

"Captain Hayes it's "a go!" This is Colonel Garron. "USA Today, CNN News, local news, and the boys at Caltech all reported an earthquake of almost 5.5 on the Richter scale. Report to me in three weeks at 1500 hours for your final briefing. During the experiment there was minimal civilian collateral damage, trailers knocked off their foundations and a few businesses lost their electrical and water service but were restored in less than a day. Overall, the damage was very minimal with no injuries or casualties. We are pleased with the results of our special top secret bunker bomb which worked out as expected. Captain this is extremely sensitive material no one not even the President or the Joint Chiefs of Staff know about this. This information is ultra-top-secret Captain Hayes. Do you understand Captain?"

"Yes sir" was Captain Hayes curt answer.

Jack Garron, now a Colonel, reflected on a singular mission he had flown with Cam Hayes, 25 years ago.

….. Flying low at treetop level as well, their evasive outer skin concealed their identity from any communist sympathizer. The plan was for Jack to be the lead aircraft to come in from the East and land at Baan Bang Rak airfield

Thailand. Using his night vision and thermal cameras, he would check for any heat blooms that may indicate hostiles in the area. Once on the ground, Jack would give the OK for Cam to land his craft. The ranger team, led by Colonel Hussein would silently proceed to the warehouse, destroy it and kill any hostiles and return to the waiting aircrafts. The raid should take no longer than forty-five minutes if all went well. Jack and Cam as well Captains Lee and Sivasambo were to stay with their respective crafts to be ready for immediate extraction after the completed mission. Before landing, Jack checked out the airfield, using his nighttime cameras and thermal imaging cameras. There was nothing to be seen his nighttime cameras did not pick up any movement and his thermal cameras did not illuminate any signature heat blooms. All seemed quiet. Jack landed his craft and radioed Cam to come on in and land next to him. Two minutes later Cam landed his craft ten meters away from Jack.

"Get ready to go, steady-lah" shouted Colonel Hussein in his Malay dialect, as he alighted from the craft and met up with the rest of his team from the two crafts.

The crossfire was murderous, white hot tracer bullets from the West and South of the airfield caught the team in a deadly crossfire. Immediately Colonel Hussein went down taking a bullet to his shoulder. Four other members of the team were cut down in seconds not to move again.

Cam shouted, "Jack it's a trap I'm going out to get Colonel Hussein."

"No Cam, this is my job" replied Jack over his headset. "I've been through this before. I am not going to let this happen again by sitting still. Give me covering fire with your nine-millimeter."

As soon as Jack jumped out his craft a rocket propelled grenade exploded hitting his craft. The explosion instantly killed Captain Lee and set the aircraft on fire. Jack was momentarily knocked down from the concussion but recovered enough to try and retrieve Captain Lee who was already dead. Captain Lee was trapped inside the burning craft. Jack could not extricate Captain Lee who was caught up in the webbing of his seat belt harness. In trying to get Captain Lee out of the burning craft Jack severely burned his hands and arms, however, it was a futile attempt as Captain Lee died in the conflagration.

"May day! May day!" Cam shouted into his headset. "We need immediate assistance at Baan Bank Rak airfield. Respond ASAP." He urgently repeated his distress call over his radio headset.

"Roger," said a friendly voice, "this is the rescue ship USS Baxter we have a chopper on the way with an ETA in ten minutes to your location."

The crossfire continued killing two more of the Malaysian Rangers who were huddled next to Cam's craft.

Cam rattled off his nine-millimeter causing a momentary suspension of incoming fire.

By this time Jack with his burned hands, along with a wounded Colonel Hussein, Captain Sivasambo and four surviving members of the assault team formed a defensive perimeter around the one intact aircraft.

"Cam! get out of here take Captain Sivasambo, Colonel Hussein and the rest of the rangers back to Kuantan," said Jack over his headset. ``

"That's a negative Jack, I'm staying until the rescue chopper gets you guys the hell outa of here. Captain

Sivasambo and I will lift off and provide covering fire with my nine-millimeter." By this time Cam knew where the incoming fire was coming from. Both he and Captain Sivasambo began to see them clearly in his night vision and thermal cameras. Before he could elevate his nose for takeoff another RPG round exploded in front of him. Bits of shrapnel pierced his windshield wounding Cam's eyes and face.

"Captain Sivasambo take over. I can't see right now." Cam shouted out as he was blinded by penetrating glass shards. Captain Sivasambo took over, he was high enough to hover and rotate his craft in various directions to provide covering fire. Captain Sivasambo did so for five minutes until he was out of ammunition. Landing again, he set his craft down by Jack's burning craft. The suppression fire seemed to have worked as incoming fire seemed to have ceased. Ten minutes seemed like a long time but the chopper from the rescue ship Baxter arrived at the airfield and sat down close to the burning craft.

"I see you guys need my help" said a medic from the USS Baxter. "We have hospital services on board, I only have room for the injured. Whoever is not hurt will have to wait for my return. "Captain Sivasambo, can you fly Cam's craft back to Kuantan along with the survivors and the dead?" said Jack.

"I believe I can, you chaps have trained me well enough by now. My concern is the broken windshield. But, If I put my helmet on and pull my visor down, I believe I can do it, and protect myself from the wind blowing in through the broken glass" as the murderous crossfire ceased. The morning sun was just beginning to rise above the horizon. The communist insurgents were pleased with the results of their ambush......

That was the last time Jack saw his aviator friend Cam Hayes; Cam resigned his position from the Army due to his injuries and became a Muslim and a dual citizen of Malaysia and the USA. He and his Malay wife settled down in Malaysia opening a beach resort with his wife near the town of Kuantan Malaysia. Jack decided to stay on to finish his career in the service teaching young flying officers how to fly helicopters at Fort Rucker. In time, after 20 years of service, Jack reached the position of Colonel in charge of flight school training at Fort Rucker.

And now Cam Hayes's son Anwar bin Hussein was sent by his Malaysian government to meet Jack Garron at Fort Rucker for an urgent top-secret assignment. The world had spun 360 degrees again. Those Indian chaps who believed in reincarnation knew what they were talking about. They had a saying "What goes around comes back at you again."

Captain Hayes and his co -pilot Lieutenant Chin both returned to their home base in Kuantan Malaysia.

"We will wait for orders from Colonel Garron and our defense minister to give us the green light to conduct our mission.

CHAPTER 9

Kuala Lumpur Malaysia

A month earlier Trenton Winchester, attached to the Malaysian Ministry of Agricultural met at the residence of Malaysia's Prime Minister Dr. Dato Haji Abu Bin Lela at his home in Federal Hill Kuala Lumpur.

"Thank you for coming all this way to meet with me," said Malaysia's Prime Minister cheerfully. "I will get straight to the point Mr. Winchester. I have information that I think you will find mutually agreeable. We have the woman that was with Kim Jung Nam the day he was assassinated. We have kept her in house arrest until we meet with you. She has valuable intelligence about North Korea for your government." Dr Abu said in a mysterious tone.

It was enough to keep Trenton Winchester intrigued.

"Why don't you deliver the woman to us now so we can determine on our own terms what sort of intelligence she may have to offer. She has had nothing at all that would be of use to us?" he said in an irritated tone.

"Well, you see Mr. Winchester, we want something from your government as well, an intriguing exchange you might say quid pro quo" said Dr Abu.

"Like what can America offer Malaysia?" Your country has everything it needs, a strong economy, money, power in Southeast Asia, a well-developed education system and respect throughout Southeast Asia," said Trenton Winchester in a matter-of-fact tone.

"Yes, indeed that is true however, those damned Chinese are building manufactured islands throughout the South China Sea. The Chinese call it a "string of pearls." They have now recently finished building an island no more than fifteen miles in international waters from our coastline at Kuala Terengganu", Dr Abu said in a hopeful tone.

In their attempt to build the artificial island as quickly as possible Beijing threatened the workers and engineers with punishment if their island was not built on schedule Consequently It was constructed carelessly and poorly. Shakily built the manufactured islands as quickly as possible building the artificial islands in order to seize territories in the South China Sea. Between 2013 and 2018 huge construction vessels pulverized reefs to create raw material for the bases. Ships that served as dredgers could shift massive amounts of cubic meters of sand per hour. In their effort to build bases, Chinese engineers destroyed the ecology of the surrounding seas, all sea life, coral, and surrounding ecology was devastated, with no plan of restoration. Their artificial island was built on compressed sand and coral but not on bedrock.

"Yes! We know about the Chinese in their attempts to control the South China Sea. Dr. Abu, we have asked the Chinese to cease and desist from building any more synthetic islands. However, our focus is directed on North Korea to stop firing those missiles over Japan. What do you want from us?".

"We want the United States to sink the island the Chinese have recently built off our Coastline. And it might be a formula for future operations in other parts of the South China Sea. Then you can have the Thai woman to glean whatever you want from her about more Korean clandestine activities," Dr Abu said in a matter-of-fact tone. "You will probably see she has a lot to offer."

"Dr. Abu this will lead to World War III, are you satisfied this is your only course of action you wish to take? The United States Government will never agree to such a stipulation Dr. Abu", he said incredulously.

"Yes, I know but I want you to hear me out first.

"First of all, that artificial island close to our coastline has been built haphazardly. Once it will be built, then the Chinese could do whatever they want, control and tax our exports for shipping, lumber, palm oil, and our fishing industry and threaten us with their military might. They are also building a runway to have immediate access to our interior as well as quicker access to our neighbors which would affect the worldwide economy and stability including yours Mr. Winchester. Now! Secondly, here is the good news you may not know about, and best of all the Chinese don't know about it as well. Our intelligence gathering ability has found out that manufactured island off our coast was built too quickly with not enough preparation time to make the island stable. The concrete revetments are crumbling The Chinese contractors hastily dredged and excavated as much coral and sand to make the manmade island but did not stabilize the underpinnings and without securing the foundations on bed rock of the island so when you walk on it certain parts of the island you can see that it is soft and a little spongy"

"So, what has that got to do with us?" said Trenton. Winchester.

"We have a chance at this moment in time to sink the island by natural means. It will be a joint covert operation obviously and it will be engineered as though mother nature did all the damage" Dr. Abu said. "China will never suspect that the United States and Malaysia had a covert hand in the sinking of their island just fifteen miles off our coast."

"How do you plan to do this? Trenton Winchester asked curiously, indicating in a tone that he was interested in Dr. Abu's plan.

"We have just recently discovered a new fault line about 1,000 feet deep on the west side on the ocean floor but close enough to be hidden from the Chinese artificial island. Currently we feel the Chinese don't know about this. It was recently discovered by one of our oceanographers, Dr Mahmut Abu Bin Lela. He graduated from one of your universities in oceanography at the Scripts Institute of Oceanography in San Diego. The Chinese Engineers did not know anything about this surprising new fault line. We also know that the United States has developed a super bunker buster bomb that can burrow itself at least five hundred feet or more under the ocean floor. The resulting explosion would be catastrophic enough providing a typical signature to activate an earthquake on the Richer Scale as a major undersea earthquake. Scientists would categorize it as an undisclosed seismic event. We would have two of our pilots Captain Hayes and Lieutenant Chin, fly your specially designed helicopter at low altitude that cannot be detected by radar and drop your special bunker buster bomb onto the sea floor directly into the fault line. If something should happen to Captain Hayes, then the Chinese would realize that his background is Malaysian not U.S. thereby exonerating your country and reducing tensions between East and West. What do you say Mr. Winchester?"

"If your pilot should get shot down then what about retribution from China to Malaysia?" said Mr. Winchester

"We will tell China our pilot was on a frequent training mission that we have done many times with no intent of any covert action. The Chinese are familiar with our frequent training flights. Allah will prevail, said Dr. Abu," hopefully said. "It is written!" Dr Abu said with finality.

"How do you know all this?" Trenton said in a surprised and astonished tone.

""We Malaysians have eyes and ears everywhere on World activities. We know many things we do not share with the world. We are cheeky bastards. The British when they occupied our country taught us very well how to be cheeky bastards, they were good at that. We love it when we can play jokes or put one over to Orang Putihs." (white people)

After the meeting with Trenton, Dr Abu called his defense minister Encik (mister) Raz.

"Listen there is more to this Thai woman than what she is telling the US. I have a feeling she is somehow connected to those Thai Pirates that have been creating havoc to our fishing fleet. I have a feeling this Thai women might be able to lead us to where the Thai Pirates have their hideout. If we are lucky, we can find them. I want to put a detail on her day and night and see where she can lead us. Is this something we can do?"

"Yes, prime minister, it will be done", said a respectful minister Raz.

Trenton Winchester presented the newfound information to the State Department who in turn shared intelligence with the Department of Defense and the President. The plan was a good one, however the President was angry why he was not informed of the experiment near Ridgecrest that caused an earthquake to the surrounding areas. Despite being close to federal land, it also caused some damage to the nearby civilian population of Ridgecrest.

"Speaking in an aggressive tone to his key members of his inner circle including the Chairperson of the Joint Chiefs of Staff began pointing his finger at everyone.

"Gentleman if this experiment ever gets out to the news media, then I am a cooked goose, I could never run for a second presidency. And you gentlemen will find your careers short-lived. Am I clear!"

"Yes Mr. President" they all said in unison like children being lectured by their school master for doing something wrong."

"Overall, I like the plan. There is no evidence of our fingerprints on the plan, let's go with it and tell the Prime Minister of Malaysia we like his plan and to give the go ahead for the Thai girl we think she has much more information about North Korea that has not been exchanged with us."

Cy Hing had been under house arrest for several weeks by Malaysian Security Police. She was not harmed but could not leave the grounds of her captive site either.

Unexpectedly a white man arrived to talk to her. Mr. Trenton Winchester from who spoke both Bahasa Malaysia and Thai fluently. Mr. Winchester began introducing himself.

I'm from the US Embassy. I came here to ask you some questions about North Korea. After we are finished then you are free to go home, we will put you on a plane and send you to Bangkok, however we may have a few more questions for you after you return home. She agreed to leave her home address and gave her address to Trenton, she was excited.

Trenton recognized that she was a brave and intelligent woman who had gone through traumatic events through no fault of her own.

Cy Hing could not believe what she was hearing, at last a chance of freedom to go home. The daily interviews lasted for five days, giving information whatever she knew to Trenton.

Kim Jong Nam had revealed to her in great deal of sensitive information about North Korea that she was glad to share with Trenton after her fifth and final day of questioning.

A week later Trenton Winchester finally addressed Cy Hing.

"Miss Hing, I think we are finished," he had gleaned a great deal of information about North Korea's intentions with more to reveal on their local stage and on the world stage, to the extent whatever Kim Jung Nam had previously told her.

"Thank you for sharing with us you have been extremely helpful. We are finished for the time being now you can return to Thailand. She had also told him how her father sold her into prostitution, and she lived as a sex worker after the typhoon hit Thailand in 2011. Trenton Winchester was very sympathetic about her plight. He felt her answers were genuine and not manufactured for his convenience.

"Neither the Malaysian authorities nor us should bother you anymore unless we may have a few more questions, Miss Hing. However, we would like to know where you are living in case something turns up. Where would you like us to take you? We will also give you some spending money for food and transportation back to Thailand."

She felt attracted to this kind American who could speak her language very well.

"I need to go back to the Hotel Lido. Can you call Mr. Singh for me if he still has my belongings so I could come and gather them up."

In a frightened tone she asked Trenton "would my meeting with you ever be revealed to North Korea, otherwise North Korean agents are bound to kill me?"

"No Miss Hing, your presence with us will never be revealed, it will be strictly confidential. OK we will call him for you so you can get your belongs."

True to his word, Trenton called the Hotel Lido and told Hardeep Singh that Cy Hing would be coming to the hotel to retrieve her belongings.

"That is wonderful news," replied Hardeep Singh, "we will have everything ready."

He quickly dialed another number.

"Hello" came a voice from the other end of the phone conversation.

"I have a girl for you, wait for my phone call. I will call you to come and get her. I want 100,000 Bhat ($2500)" Agreed "said the other voice.

Kuantan, Malaysia

Colonel Garron met with Captain Hayes and his co-pilot Lieutenant Chin in Kuantan Malaysia briefing them on their pending mission. It was the same airbase that he and Captain Hayes's father had taken off from for their clandestine assault in Thailand 20 years earlier.

"OK, here is your briefing on your mission Captain Hayes. You have been trained long enough to fly one of our super-duper modified helicopters, the ones your father and I used to fly many years ago. We need a Chinese Malaysian pilot in case you are downed so there would be no connection to the United States. On the 23rd of July you will take off from our airbase in Kuantan. With your co-pilot Captain Chin to help with navigation. Even if you do get detected by radar your craft's super sensitive skin will disguise your presence as a flock of birds. You will fly at treetop level so you will eliminate any likelihood of getting picked up by Chinese Radar. Look for a horseshoe shaped island about 5 miles long due East from Kuala Terengganu. You will head for the island about 15 miles East of the Kuala Terengganu City; it doesn't even have a name. Your craft will be carrying a unique bunker buster bomb, and we want you to drop that bomb at the precise coordinates we'll give to Lieutenant Chin."

"What is so special about the bomb?" asked Lieutenant Chin.

"Lieutenant, the less you know about that bomb the better off you will be in case you are captured by the Chinese."

"Is it a nuclear bomb?" asked Lieutenant Chin, with a degree of uncertainty in his voice."

"No! " And get that notion out of your head Lieutenant. Once you drop that bomb, immediately turn around and go back to Kuantan, your mission will be over. Dust off is at 09:30 hours on July 23rd. Good luck with your mission. Here are your orders: read them and then destroy them."

Captain Hayes and his copilot took their orders. Obligated to complete their mission but content not to probe any more. He and his co-pilot for the first time saw together this huge corkscrew shaped bomb attached to the underbelly of his helicopter as one complete attack unit.

"Just what the hell is that?" said his co-pilot" as they both looked at the corkscrewed shaped bunker buster bomb, and they want us to drop it into the ocean and not on land." exclaimed his copilot, in astonishment.

"Never mind, let's get the job done." Said Captain Hayes with a serious note in his voice.

Kuala Lumpur

"I do have the girl," Hardeep Singh reiterated over the phone. "You can have her for MR2,000 ($2400). I hear that Chinese workers are lonely for the companionship for women. You should be able to make a lot of money. He was talking to Thai Pirates.

Since the fall of South Vietnam by North Viet Communists ocean going sea pirates have been praying on the exodus of Vietnamese boat people fleeing South Vietnam to find a safer haven from South Vietnam. Based on various locations along coastal waters pirates from Thailand found Vietnamese Boat people were easy prey. Robbing, pillaging, murdering, and raping were the clandestine and nefarious activities of the Thai pirates. Especially lucrative were taking Vietnamese women into forced prostitution sold into brothels controlled by the pirates.

Aizoon the leader of the local band of Thai Pirates knew he could get a lot more than MR 2,000 than what he paid for Cy Hing.

Cy Hing prepared to enter the taxi thinking she was being taken to the Thai embassy and then eventually provide a way of getting home to Thailand. Before she could get into the taxi from out of nowhere a hood was placed over her head and her hands were quickly bound.

"Call me again," Aisoon said to Hardeep Singh while shaking his hand. "Here is your money. If you should find a Malay women, I would pay a lot more. I hear these Islamic women go wild once they are released from their sexual suppression."

"Yes, that is fine, answered Hardeep Singh, but you will find Indian women they are the most skilled in sex. You will get your money's worth from your customers. They will leave you begging for more boasted Hardeep Singh."

Of course, nothing is further from the truth men love to embellish fantasies from gossip heard in bars boasting and fantasizing about the sexual mores of women passed on from man to man Of course, nothing was further from the truth no one was correct, prostitution is still prostitution it is a demeaning transitional act without any love or caring, only sex for money debasing and degrading females which often lead to violence and sometimes death.

Cy Hing was thrust into the taxi sitting on the back seat with an unknown assailant. For 10 hours she sat there with no food or water. Bound and blindfolded She was allowed to relieve herself once the taxi entered a secluded jungle area. Once reaching the seaside port of Kuala Terengganu she was thrust into a sampan along with four other women Finally her hood was removed and the shackles that bound her hands were released.

Bruce Chan received an anxious phone call from Dr Abu.

"Bruce, I have some sad news for you. Since you stopped asking her questions, we have had someone follow her in case something extraordinary should happen to her before she returns to Negri Siam (Bahasa Malaysia's word for Thailand) Your Thai woman Cy Hing has been kidnapped right outside the Hotel Lido. One of our men followed the car all the way to Kuala Terengganu. From there she was thrown along with four other women into a motorized sampan heading for the Chinese island. We think she will be forced into prostitution again. We have five days before we initiate our mission to sink the island. With the resulting earthquake she will be killed along with the other four women," said Dr Abu dramatically. "What can you do in so short a time?"

"I need to talk to my President first to see what our options may be," he said curtly, thank you for calling me." Hanging up the phone quickly.

The next day Bruce Chan met the President in the White House, "Mr. President Bruce started. "We have some disturbing news that our informant on North Korea has been kidnapped by Thai Pirates and taken to the island we plan to sink in 4 days. Can we do something to help Cy Hing?" pleaded Bruce she has been very valuable to us."

"Like what! We only have four days before our mission with Malaysia" the President said with a frown on his face.

"Before coming to your office, I thought about an Ad Hoc plan. We have Trenton Winchester over there in Malaysia. He is an ex-Navy Seal. Let's give him the OK to see if he could rescue Cy Hing and perhaps the other captive four ladies. It would be strictly voluntary and up to him, but I feel he can improvise a plan to get that island" Bruce said hopefully.

The President replied, "It will be up to him, however, should he get captured by the Chinese we will disavow of any knowledge of his activities. I also have told Dr Abu that I will be coming to Kuala Lumpur to help celebrate Malaysian Independence Day."

"Thank you Mr. President I will notify Trenton immediately to devise an Ad Hoc plan to help get Cy Hing and the other ladies off that island," he said gratefully.

On phone call Trenton can you produce a plan to rescue those ladies off that Chinese island.

"You are an ex - Navy Seal. Can you, do it can you improvise a plan? You now have less than 3 days to get to that island before we sink it. You are on your own. There is one caveat, however. Our President will disavow any knowledge of your activities. The plan is strictly voluntarily. The President is also planning to arrive in Kuala Lumpur to help celebrate Malaysia's Independence Day with Malaysia's Prime Minister, the same day we sink that island. Can you, do it?" You have about three days to produce a plan. But you are not obligated to fulfil this mission."

"I'll do my best" is all he said and then hung up the phone.

Trenton made his way to Kuala Terengganu by riding MARA the Malaysian bus after system Arriving the next day he made his way down to the wharf. Spotting a fisherman who had just returned with his small catch he asked him if he could charter his boat for a one-way trip to the within 1 mile of the Chinese island. He would pay him MR 1500 Malaysian Ringgits. The fisher man needed a new engine as his old one was constantly failing. Trenton was dressed in a T shirt, shorts and around his waist hung a knife and a 45 caliber pistol.

The fisher man was impressed how well Trenton could speak Bahasa Malaysia. He had never met a Orang Putih (white person) who could speak his language so well.

"Yes", he eagerly replied for MR 1500 ringgits I could buy a new engine. It was too good to pass over, besides, it was only a one-way trip. Trenton looked harmless enough.

Within a mile off the island jumped overboard to begin swimming to the entrance of the island. He watched as the fisher man turned around to return to the mainland knowing somehow, he must somehow evacuate safely with Cy Hing and the other kidnapped women. The one thing he did not worry about was hypothermia. Malaysian waters are famous for its 80 degrees temperature or more and so he began swimming to the island 2 hours later. Being an ex-Navy seal swimming came easily to him by this time he had less than a half day to set his plan in motion. Approaching dockside, he was able to spot a half dozen small motorboats tied up in their jetties. He hoped they still had their Keyes in their ignitions. Who would have wanted to steal motorboats on this small island so far away from the Malaysian Coastline.

Captain Hayes and Lieutenant Chin were ready to lift off.

"'Allah surely is a wonderful god" Captain Hayes thought to himself. "Here I am repeating what my father and Colonel Garron did 20 years ago."

The sea was like glass with diamonds shining on the ripples making it serene and inspiring that makes the East Coast of Malaysia so famous. By tradition Fishing boats found their way on the daily morning breeze leaving on the morning tide with their jib and mainsails billing in the gentle morning breeze

Cy Hing was seated at the rear of the motorized sampan. She was back to being a prostitute again at the hands of that Thai Pirate Aisoon. and Hardeep Singh Once again she will be sold to the highest bidder on that man made built island, clutching her amulet she prayed again to Buddha.

"Hear me four quarters of the world I am butt a relative
Give me strength to walk the soft earth.
Give me eyes to see and the strength to understand.
Look upon these faces of children without numbers.
That they face the winds and walk the good road on the
day of quiet.
Lord Buddha, please release me from these shackles that
bind my soul."

At their appointed time, Captain Hayes lifted off from Kuantan and headed for the semicircular island off the coast of Malaysia. Flying erratically at 1,200 feet above the deck, heading over the eastern coastline and then over to Kuala Terengganu. Captain Hayes passed over his parent's vacation hotel providing him with a grin of satisfaction.

15 minutes later the Chinese manmade island came into view. A flat large crescent shaped island large enough to accommodate an air strip, marine docks for large ocean-going vessels as well as numerous workstations, supplies and outbuildings for workers and engineers and eating facilities. As predicted the low flying irregular shaped helicopter did show up on Chinese radar as a flock of birds.

"Ok Captain, Lieutenant Chin said, "We are to fly on the west side of the island a mile out and then electronically arm the fuse and hopefully drop the bomb from our undercarriage."

"Colonel Wong!" shouted the startled and curios Chinese cadre, "look at that funny looking helicopter it's getting too close,"

"It must be those crazy Malay pilots who do not know what they are doing. They can't even fly correctly. Look how sloppily they fly their craft, up, down left right they can't even fly in a straight line otherwise, we would have picked them up on radar and our intelligence told us that Malaysia is too weak to be a threat to us. Not to worry their military is disorganized with outdated ordinance left over from the British days they are no threat to us. They are not as skilled as our own pilots," he said boasting to his junior officers and men.

"Bombs away!" shouted Lieutenant Chin at the designated IP point. "How long will it take?" he asked Captain Hayes.

"I've been told the bomb will bury itself deep into the ocean floor maybe a thousand feet deep close to the undersea fault line that the Chinese don't know about and then explode after two hours. It will give us plenty of time to get away so the explosion will not be associated with us."

Trenton slinked from building to building. What he did not know was that the heavy machinery used in developing the island and waiting for their exhausted amount of diesel fuel. So, the workers slept in and ate their morning breakfast later in the morning. Only the cooks were up, and they were not paying attention to outside activities.

After an hour creeping from building to building he eventually saw the open-air cage where Cy Hing and the other hostages were held. Using his knife, he could not pry open the pad lock open that locked the door to the open cage. The cage was open air so all the hostages were on display to incite the appetites of the Chinese workers so they could fantasize which women they would want to the highest bidder.

"Cy Hing come here," he whispered as she was overjoyed to see him, "have your female hostages take off their sarongs including yours give me all of your sarongs" he said urgently.

Puzzled by such a strange request she told the other hostages to take off their sarongs, they all took off their sarongs, standing naked not knowing what to do. They handed Trenton their sarongs. Trenton wrapped the sarongs around the muzzle of his .45 pistol making an improvised silencer. He told them to stand back as he fired into the padlock splitting it in two. The sound was muffled enough not to disturb the Chinese workers.

"Hurry! He said urgently to Cy Hing put your sarongs back on and follow me down to the jetty. From there we will find a motorboat."

As he expected, the keys were still in the ignition.

The first three boats still had their keys in them but would not start from the lack of gasoline. Finally, the fourth boat started and with all aboard they motored out of the jetty. Trenton knew he was out of time he was still 15 miles from the Malaysian Coastline.

At the same time the bomb blew up under the sea the Presidents plane touched down in Kuala Lumpur's airport.

As predicted the bomb corkscrewed itself into the soft ocean floor exactly on the unsuspected fault line and exploded after two hours. The island shook with the ferocity of a 5.5 earthquake on the Richter scale. Buildings toppled, and then a seismic wave about 5 feet tall washed onto the island devastating all the buildings, the airstrip and oceans docks. Best of all the earthquake shook the poorly and hastily built underpinnings. Slowly the island began to sink and after four hours it was completely rendered uninhabitable as it gurgled below the ocean's surface. Its foundations could no longer support the island. Those workers and engineers that survived the tsunami clung on to floatable devices as they were swept out to sea.

The undersea explosion had caused a large powerful tsunami wave traveling at a high rate of speed. There was no surface explosion as a huge spray might indicate some sort of explosive device. As the wave traveled through the sea it overtook smaller waves absorbing the energy of the smaller and slower waves making it even larger and faster.

"Look Shouted Cy Hing!" At a huge wave, it's coming right for us and it's so fast", Cried out Cy Hing. It took only a moment to capsize the motorboat all the passengers of the small boat were thrown into the sea.

Captain Hayes and Lieutenant Chin received a phone call from the prime minister and Malaysia's defense minister after they had returned to their base in Kuantan.

"Well done gentleman Allah is great, you have done your jobs well, those Chinese pariahs are no longer a threat to our coastline. Praise be to Allah they are no longer there. That Chinese manufactured island sank within four hours taking everything with it including those Thai Pirates.. That bomb you dropped eliminated the island but left an inordinate amount of debris but never mind the ocean and time will clean it up. Unfortunately, I cannot announce our participation to our country. We must keep this operation secret otherwise we will receive heavy reprisals from China. If they believe it was an underground earthquake or a sea anomaly, then we will be safe. I will let Colonel Garron know however I'm sure he knows as American satellite photos will reveal the disappearance of that manmade virus. Our operation can be used elsewhere and eliminate those treacherous chains of pearls that China is developing throughout the South China Sea."

Colonel Garron was totally aware of the success and pointed this out to the President and the Joint Chiefs of Staff in a top-secret meeting of the success of their black op's operation. All knew this was ultra top secret and could not be revealed publicly. Seismic monitors even in China demonstrated that there was a large undersea seismic earthquake off the Malaysian coast.

CHAPTER 10

South China Sea

20 miles from the Malaysian Coast

Cy Hing and Trenton had been drifting for three days away from the Malaysian coastline. Both Cy Hing and Trenton were clutching on for dear life to their wooden upside-down boat. The other women were nowhere to be found, they could not swim. By the end of the third day Cy Hing was very weak and dehydrated. The salt water burned her nose and eyes. She was tired and thirsty and could no longer hang onto her wooden boat much longer. The water became choppy and overwhelmed her, burning her nose and mouth with the salty water. She wanted to let go but seeing sharks circling around her she held on for dear might. However, at this time they did not attack. She thought of her mother how she had died from the bite of a Cobra. Would the same happen to her except for the bite of a shark?

Cy Hing I'm coming" he yelled. Grabbing her with one arm around her waist and holding on with the other, he managed to Cy Hing stay afloat.

"Hey, grab a rope," said a voice. A large Thai fishing boat had seen the upside-down boat with Cy Hing drifting lifelessly while she was still clutching her wooden boat. Cy Hing did not respond, nor did she try to grab the rope. One of the boat's The crew member who threw her the rope dove into water and tied the rope around Ct Hing's waist.

59

"Pull hard! He yelled at his crew while keeping an eye on the circling sharks.

The crew pulled Cy Hing onto the deck of the large fishing boat who remained semi unconscious.

"It's a man and a woman!" the five-member crew gasped. The crewman who had tied the rope to Cy Hing came on board and looked at Cy Hing.

"I know this woman," he shouted in a surprised tone.

"Who is she?" the crew said in unison.

"She is my sister," came his amazed answer.

"Cy Hing wake up, wake up it's me your brother Natthakit"

Cy Hing's mind was still numb and very weak, but the name of her elder brother brought her around to her senses.

"Natthakit is it really you," she said in bewilderment "How did you get here and how did you find me?"

"When our father sold you into prostitution, with the money he earned from selling you he re assembled our lives and also, we were able to rejuvenate our rice paddies. The big storm that destroyed our lives as we know of it eventually provided much needed soil, mud, and nutrients to our rice paddies. We did not need to buy any fertilizer. Subsequently over the last several years we have had huge bumper crops and earned surplus money. With the surplus money our father bought a fishing boat to supply that Chinese island with various supplies of rice, water, seafood, and vegetables. The contract we had with the Chinese increased our money supply even more. The Chinese paid well for their supplies. They gave us a nice contract to supply them on a weekly basis. We don't know why but now we see the island is gone. Last year our father died of something called Covid 19. He painfully regretted selling you. It's not what he wanted to do but he knew he had to do it to salvage the rest of our family. With the surplus money we bought our fishing boat so we would not be so dependent on our rice crops if bad weather hit us again. We all missed you so much Cy Hing we did not know where you went so, we could not find you. Come with me and meet the rest of our family. It has been a long time for all of us.

On their way back to Thailand Cy Hing told her the story to Natthakit what happened to her until the time he found her drifting in the sea. They were very grateful to Trenton for saving their sister. She couldn't wait to see her homeland again and the rest of her family.

CHAPTER 11

Washington DC

Bruce Chan was pleased with the information gleaned from Cy Hing by Trenton Winchester about North Korean political and military activities. Trenton had come back to Washington to meet with officials at the State Dept

"So that woman who accompanied Kim Jung Nam was a prostitute and his traveling companion."

"Yes Bruce, from what I could tell Kim Jung Nam was a good guy, he was on his brother's hit list."

"Why?"

"He was against his brother's firing rockets over Japan and draining the county's reserves on militarizing his country's assets instead of providing North Korea with food, medical care, education proper housing and bringing North Korea into contemporary standards."

"We knew that China was North Korea's benefactor and now we understand even better why North Korea keeps firing missiles over Japan. However, the Chinese have slowed down their island building activities as the world community is now aware, and it seems one of their islands actually sunk. The science community thinks it was an undersea quake. So, there is some paranoia in the Chinese government. They seem to think it might happen again to their other islands. Whether China will attack Taiwan is anyone's question. Only time will tell."

"Bruce, I want you to know that Cy Hing was sold and forced into prostitution by her father. That big storm that hit Thailand several years ago devastated Cy Hing's family. Selling her into prostitution was the only way her father could save his family. I think she was a brave woman. In her own way she and Kim Jung Nam also tried to help the West and freedom of the press by releasing overly sensitive information about North Korea. Is there anything we can do to help her?"

"Let me see what I can do" said Bruce Chan, "I understand your concerns."

"Hello Minister Mohamad Raz," Bruce Chan said on a secure phone line. How are you doing my old friend?"

"Ah Bruce it has been many years since you were a Peace Corp volunteer teacher at Sekolah (school) Galing in Kuantan and I was the headmaster there, I am fine Bruce. What can I do for you Bruce that deserves a long overdue phone call from you" with a scornful tone in his voice.

"I know those Thai Pirates will occasionally rob your fishing boats and hamper your fishing fleet. I know they are always looking for women to kidnap, especially Malay and Vietnamese Women. However, they are hard to find because they hide out in Thailand's thick jungle. Well, I have a little bit of news for you that you might find interesting. The manager at the Hotel Lido in Brickfields is also a sympathizer for those Thai Pirates he receives gratuities for useful bits of information that he can pass on to the Pirates and sometimes China. He is an Indian chap by the name of Hardeep Singh, he also may be leaking hard intelligence to China as to what Malaysia knows regarding building that manmade island off the coast of Terengganu. Why don't you pay him a visit?

"Bruce, I will investigate it, thank you for the tip. I want you to come back to Malaysia for Hari Raya (Independence Day). We can have a great feast together with my family."

"If your wife will cook curry ayam (chicken curry) then I am already getting my plane tickets. I can't wait to taste it again. Inshallah," said Bruce.

"God willing Bruce," replied Mohamad Raz

CHAPTER 12

Kuala Lumpur's Correctional Facility

"We have him" said constable Ah Hing with pride and authority. He was surprised but showed no resistance. We searched his premises, but we did not find any weapons.

"Well lucky for him if we had found any weapons he would be in jail for life or even executed," said the officer of the day. "Let's interrogate him now so he knows how strict and efficient Malaysian law is," he was thinking of a promotion he might receive.

"What is your name?" said the constable from the Malaysian security forces in a very harsh tone to his captor

"My name is Hardeep Singh. Why am I here, I have done nothing wrong?"

"What is your nationality and where were you born?" said the scornful Malaysian police constable.

"I am a Malaysian citizen. I was born in Ipoh, Malaysia. I am Indian by birth."

The constable continued, "We are arresting you for conspiring and seditious activities against the Malaysian Government. You are being charged for providing information to those Thai Pirates as well as providing information to the government of China."

Hardeep Singh knew these were serious charges and meant the death penalty by hanging if found guilty.

"Mr. Singh, if you tell us what we want to know, we can be lenient with you. In the spirit of Deepavali (Indian religious holiday) you will suffer a caning of ten lashes as your punishment and then let you go, how does that sound?"

Hardeep Singh thought about his choices, the possibility of hanging or ten lashes with the rotan (cane) providing he tells what he knows to the interrogation officer.

"OK I will tell you what I want you to know and receive my punishment of ten lashes of the rotan." I don't want to die!"

The next morning Hardeep Singh was taken to a different cell especially equipped for caning. With both hands and feet shackled by a chain to the wall and stripped completely naked he laid prone on the caning table he waited for his 10 lashes to his back.

As the police constable was about to begin the caning to Hardeep's back the officer in charge halted the proceedings.

"Wait just one moment, said an officer while raising his hand, "I want to dip the cane in urine." Talking to the police constable "You know we used to use horse urine. In the past horse urine was very potent and often killed the person from severe infection after the use of the rotan. Now we use human urine, it is not as strong as horse urine but will equally provide a serious and painful infection as a lasting memory to his actions."

Hardeep was caned 10 times and screamed as each whip tore through the tissues of his back. He passed out from the tearing of his skin as it left long blood stained wounds from his flogging. His blood and chunks of partially torn flesh cascaded from his back dripping onto the floor, he did not know about the rotan dipped in urine. Malaysian justice is very swift and effective despite to eliminate his agony to let his captors know how effective their caning was. Hardeep told as much as he knew about his clandestine activities to the delight and eagerness of his Malaysian Captors. Despite confessing, the flogging was still metered out

"Take him back to the infirmary until he recovers and then let him go if he does not die first," said the officer.

After the 14th day Hardeep returned to the Hotel Lido. His painful back was not healing well. It was burning and was causing him to run a fever. He was constantly sweating, soiling his shirt with pus, blood and sweat. His infections from the urine caused him to be in constant pain. It was Deepavali and he wanted to return to his home in Ipoh to enjoy Deepavali festivities with his family despite his injuries.

"Did you put the tracking device on his car so that we know where he is at all times?" said defense Minister Mohamad Hassan to Inspector Mahmut in charge of police in Kuala Lumpur. "We want to eliminate him as expeditiously as possible," said the defense minister.

"Why not just shoot him and get it over with?" said inspector Mahmut.

"Because if we shoot him the whole Indian community will be outraged. Because it is only the police and military who carry firearms. The civilian population is not allowed to carry weapons of any kind. The evidence of a shooting will eventually point back to us. I have a better way to dispose of him.

"Captain Hayes, do you still have the capability to use that helicopter you used on that mission to that Chinese Island?"

"Yes sir, why do you ask?"

"I have something special for you to do. Here are your orders." His name is Hardeep Singh, he is an insurgent and can't be allowed to function anymore in our country. We believe tomorrow morning he will be driving to Ipoh for Deepavali to spend time with his family. We have a tracking device hidden in his car. Once underway you will be alerted to follow him on the road to Ipoh. You will find him easy to track because your tracking instruments will signal you coming from his tracking device. At the appropriate moment we want you to drop a low load napalm bomb onto his car causing it to crash and go up in flames so that it looks like is a civilian motor accident. The Indian population will understand that it was just another auto accident as there are many accidents on that high fatality dangerous two-lane road between Kuala Lumpur and Ipoh."

The following morning Captain Hayes conducted his orders as requested by his defense minister. With great precision Hardeep Sing was eliminated from the Malaysian population. Once again it was a clandestine operation. No one was the wiser.

Pyongyang, Korea
July 2023

Minister Hui Bing Low was a lower ranking case officer from the ministry that came to Korea without an entourage. He had set up a meeting with Kim Jung Un to discuss current affairs.

"Thank you for allowing me to meet with Supreme Leader of North Korea. This is my first time meeting you."

"Yes, it is my pleasure to meet with you as well. What brings you to Korea?" he replied in an irritated tone. He was annoyed that a lower ranking case officer from the Chinese delegation was sent to talk to him. He was even without a political portfolio.

"Supreme leader," he began, "The times have changed since we talked with you many years ago. You were able to provide us a smoke screen for us while we supplied you with military equipment and supplies for your rockets and missiles while we built our secret manmade islands throughout the South China Sea. The ruse worked very well, and we were able to build at least seven islands throughout the South China Sea.

"Yes, I know that already, why are you telling me something I already know?"

"Because most of the global countries are totally against us now, even the international courts have ruled against us regarding those islands as our claim to our own sovereign domain. At one time when Europe was a dark hell hole, and the United States did not even exist we explored the South China Sea claiming Taiwan and other islands we discovered as part of Chinese sovereignty. At this present time, our economy is not as strong as it used to be. We have loaned Russia billions in weapons in their fight against Ukraine. Worst of all our islands were poorly planned already, the concrete sea revetments are crumbling from the high tides we did not anticipate. Our runways are cracking and need to be constantly repaired daily. Even walking on some parts of our island it's as if you're walking on a sponge,"

"So, what has that got to do with my country?" Already he knew what the answer was going to be.

"Supreme leader, we have spent billions on those islands. We also realize that we have walked into a trap."

"How is that?" Jim Jung Un asked inquisitively.

"We now realize that if the West and its allies decide to declare war on our islands, they would have an easy stationary targets. Our missiles, radar operations ships, dry docks and other strategic assets would be easy targets. Nothing is mobile or elusive; everything is a fixed target. We can't hide anything. Nothing could be hidden below sea level. So, we are slowing down our efforts to make additional synthetic islands. As a result, we are not able to send you very much military hardware for your missile program as we have done before. Already the world and the UN know about our efforts it is no longer a secret to deflect criticism back to you. Your smoke screen operations are no longer vital to us. However, if you wish to fire an ICBM or two to keep South Korea on its toes then that is up to you, but we no longer will be sending you supplies for you missiles program."

Kim Jong Un was devastated he had always depended on China for its rich resources. It meant now he would have to dip into his own country's meager resources. Already he was beginning to see how poor their own social situation and internal infrastructures had become.

"Very well, minister Hui Bing Low, please tell your supreme leader my debt of gratitude and that I understand the situation well." said North Korea's beloved leader.

Kim Jung Un eventually realized he was sleeping with a snake. He realized what ever China had sent him in the way of aid would somehow need to be paid in return. The Chinese are shrewd enough to want a return on their investment Trillions of dollars. He had walked into his own trap. He had no idea how he could ever repay back the Chinese Government.

It was a slowing of the missile program and also the end of the manufactured islands that China thought that they could deceive the world and hold South East Asia hostage. Evidence seemed to show that the concrete underpinnings and foundations were beginning to fail. Stress from the weight of tons of sand, concrete and coral stone were compressing the flooring even more than anticipated causing many of the islands to slowly begin sinking.

Bangkok, Thailand

Cy Hing was overjoyed to see her brothers again, as they were to see her the youngest had joined the military while another brother managed the rice fields. Her eldest brother is the one who rescued here on his fishing boat. Her family has come a long way since that dreadful hurricane so many years ago. Cy Hing needed to decide what to do with her life. Looking back on her life there is something she must do. It hit her like the typhoon that destroyed their lives.

Placing a newspaper ad in the Bangkok Chronicle she chose the Bangkok Chronicle it reads in both English and Thai:

"Women of Thailand! We must stop the sexual exploitation of our women.

It is degrading and shameful.

We mut petition our government to put a stop the selling our women,

like worthless dogs. Meet me on Tuesday at the Chao Phyra River Restaurant

if you want to meet me to put help then let's put a union together to partition our government to stop prostitution at 11:00 am."

A week later, Cy Hing arrived at the Chao Praya River Restaurant to plead her case to the few women who showed up. Of notice was a lady by the name of Flint who was also trying to petition her Thai government to stop the sexual exploitation of women. After the meeting, Flint wanted to meet with Cy Hing.

"Yes, Cy I also have been trying to stop human trafficking as well, but I have run into many obstacles. I need money which I do not have to donate to political contributions or bribe officials of their respective political parties. Even the King will endorse us providing we donate money to his own political agenda. Right now, the doors are not open for me. Our government knows they can lose a lot of money from tax revenues even though prostitution is against the law."

"I have money," Cy Hing blurted out. I can give you some money. I know where to get it," she said triumphantly. Can you meet me here next week at 11am at this restaurant I will give you money all that you need for your organization."

"Thank you. Yes, this will be an unexpected gift from the Buddha," Flint replied in happily.

"Until next week" they both replied to each other.

Cy Hing had remembered the bank account that Kim Jung Nam had told her before his death. She remembered the name of the bank and the account number. Kim Jung Nam had seen that Cy Hing's name was on the bank account. He did this before he was assassinated in Kuala Lumpur's airport.

The next day she went to the Bank of BBL Pharate in Bangkok and as allowed to, she withdrew close to Bhat 500,000. She was overjoyed and could not wait to give the money to Flint for her campaign against prostitution. She was overwhelmed with happiness.

"Buddha is a wonderful spirit" she said to herself as she clutched her amulet.

As agreed, Cy Hing went to the Chao Praya River early and stood at the water's edge in silence with an envelope of money for Flint clenched tightly in her hands. She watched the slowly moving and gurgling river as though it was talking to her. The river was calling out to her with eddies and flotsam. A closer look at the river showed how dirty and muddy it was. Staring at the river she reflected on her life's journey. It was like a river full of tragic events. The hurricane, death of her mother, being sold into prostitution, and the severe rape she experienced, the freedom to go Chang Mai and meeting with Kim Jung Nam, the assassination in Kuala Lumpur and being on the run again only to be sold into prostitution by a treacherous and greedy hotel operator. By Buddha's blessing to be rescued by her brother after nearly drowning in the South China Sea. Her life was a cascade of fates from one climactic event to another and now back with her family. Now she was able to do some good. She felt marvelous.

"You bitch" he cried aloud. He grabbed Cy Hing around her head squeezing as hard as he could,

"I have finally found you, he shouted and spitting directly to her face."

"Who are you?" as she was barely able to get it out of her painful head.

"Don't you remember me? I was little when you last saw me, I am Fu Lei's son. You caused him great harm and suffering. I will do the same to you." He had seen Cy Hing's ad in the newspaper and so he eventually knew where to find her.

She did remember Kim Jung Nam hitting Mr. Fu Lai on the head with a frying pan at Mrs. Ananya's restaurant and the flogging she received at Mrs. Ananya's restaurant.

"Yesterday he died in great pain. I have never forgotten what you did to him. Now I will do the same to you," pulling out a tire iron from his belt and before Cy Hing could plead for mercy he struck her on the head. The gash on her head was severe.

At this time, another typhoon was approaching Thailand it was Typhoon Talim with wind gusts of 140kph. Its howling winds came ashore before the main eye hit Thailand. The winds were so strong that it snapped branches or caused tree limbs to violently bend and twist from the baying and barking winds. On one of the trees that Cy Hing and Fu Lei's son were standing under, was a Malayan Pit Viper which was feasting on small birds and rodents that were living in the tree. With a violent gust the highly poisonous snake fell out of the tree and landed on Fu lei's shoulder. The Pit Viper savagely struck Fu Lei in the neck repeatedly several times with copious amounts of venom. The venom coursed its way into his brain and heart he died very quickly as he toppled into the murky river. Appropriately the murky and dirty river reached out to him cradling him never to be seen again,

Flint arrived in time to see CY Hing with a bleeding head wound. She helped Cy Hing to her home where she cleaned and dressed her head wound.

Cy Hing became grateful to have for a close friend who came at the right time to help Cy Hing With the money she withdrew from the bank that Kim Jung Nam had told her. Both Flint and Cy Hing waged a campaign against the Thai Government to outlaw and terminate prostitution, as well as allowing same sex marriages. It was a wish fulfilled she had once told her self-many years ago.

With demanding work both Flint and Cy Hing were able to table with the Thai government their concerns. And so, in April 2023 the government of Thailand did change the laws regarding prostitution, it legalized prostitution it so that sex workers could now receive social benefits from the government. It also allowed sex workers to work legally with a government ID card saying they were sex workers allowing them free checkups at hospitals and clinics for infections from sexually transmitted diseases. The Thai government could still to keep coffers filled with tax revenues and allowed prostitutes a margin of safety. Thailand's House of Representatives did also legalize same sex marriage in Thailand.

Both Cy Hing and Flint were incredibly happy with the challenging work they fought so hard to change Thai Laws. Cy Hing felt warm and happy that she had fulfilled a wish she made to herself many years ago, despite a continuous retinue of cascading fates that controlled her life.

On one special day it was Songkran a celebration of the King's birthday, came a surprise visitor.

"Well, hello there" said a kind and familiar voice. It was Trenton Winchester.

"I have been looking for you, you can be a hard woman to find these days. I remember the address you gave me when I first saw you. It was Trenton who had rescued her from that Thai Pirate and saved from drowning when their capsized boat flipped over from the tsunami.

"Cy Hing, I have been reassigned to the Thai Embassy here in Bangkok. I want to know if you will let me see you," he said hopefully. "It has been a long time since we were swimming in the South China Sea together."

Surprised at seeing Trenton at her home "Yes, you can" she said shyly. I also have learnt how to be a stronger swimmer since my brother now owns a fishing boat and may sink in a typhoon. He stayed for supper as she cooked her favorite meal of chicken curry for him a specialty, she had learned years ago at Mrs. Anaya's restaurant. One year later Trenton Winchester and Cy Hing were married in a Buddhist temple. Trenton restored her dignity and love of life and Buddha.

"Thank you, Lord Buddha, for answering my prayers. I do not hate any one I am only seeking harmony and peace as I travel through this life. I think I have found what I have been looking for."

Epilog

It does not matter who answers our prayers. It could be Allah, Mohammad, Buddha, Jehovah, Jesus, or our Christian God. Our prayers are always answered from the people with love in their hearts.

Our holy and many of our divine spirits answer all our prayers but not in ways we expect them. It is how we travel through life never knowing what fate or our answers to prayers have in store for us.